漂鳥集〈全新插畫雙語版〉

泰戈爾／著　伍晴文／譯

Stray Birds

By Rabindranath Tagore

好讀出版

001
夏天的漂鳥，來到我窗前歌唱，又飛走了。
而秋天的黃葉，無歌歡唱，輕嘆一聲，飄落在地。

002
喔，這群世上的小小流浪者啊，
請將你們的足跡留在我的字裡行間！

001 Stray birds of summer come to my window to sing and fly away.
And yellow leaves of autumn, which have no songs,
flutter and fall there with a sigh.

002 O Troupe of little vagrants of the world,
leave your footprints in my words.

003 The world puts off its mask of vastness to its lover.
It becomes small as one song, as one kiss of the eternal.

004 It is the tears of the earth
that keep her smiles in bloom.

005 The mighty desert is burning for the love of a blade of grass
who shakes her head and laughs and flies away.

003
世界向它的愛人，卸下它巨大的面具。
它變得小如一首歌，如一個永恆之吻。

004
是大地的淚珠，
讓她的微笑一直綻放著。

005
浩瀚的大漠，對一葉綠草燃起熱烈愛火，
而她卻搖了搖頭，笑著飛走了。

006
你若因為錯過太陽而哭瞎了眼，
那你也將錯過星群。

007
舞動的流水啊，
途中的泥沙正乞求你的歌聲與流動。
你是否願意挾起不良於行的泥沙前行俱下？

006 If you shed tears when you miss the sun,
you also miss the stars.

007 The sands in your way beg for your song and your movement,
dancing water. Will you carry the burden of their lameness?

008 Her wistful face haunts my dreams
like the rain at night.

009 Once we dreamt that we were strangers.
We wake up to find that we were dear to each other.

010 Sorrow is hushed into peace in my heart
like the evening among the silent trees.

008
她熱切的容顏，
宛如夜晚的雨滴，纏擾我夢。

009
我們曾夢見彼此陌路。
醒來時才發現，我們本是親密無間。

010
在我心中業已歸於平靜的憂傷，
宛如降落在寂林中的夜幕。

011
一些看不見的手指，像慵懶的微風，
在我心弦彈奏著篇篇樂章。

012
「喔，大海啊，您說的是什麼話語？」
「是永恆的疑問。」
「喔，穹空啊，您的回答又是什麼？」
「是永恆的沉默。」

011 Some unseen fingers, like an idle breeze,
are playing upon my heart the music of the ripples.

012 "What language is thine, O Sea?"
"The language of eternal question."
"What language is thy answer, O Sky?"
"The language of eternal silence."

013 Listen, my heart,
to the whispers of the world with which it makes love to you.

014 The mystery of creation is like the darkness of night — it is great.
Delusions of knowledge are like the fog of the morning.

015 Do not seat your love upon a precipice
because it is high.

013
聽著，我心，
聽那世界的呢喃，它正在向你示愛呀。

014
造物的奧祕，彷似夜之闇黑如許偉大。
知識卻猶如晨霧般虛幻。

015
莫因峭壁高聳，
而將你的愛情置之於上。

016 I sit at my window this morning
where the world like a passer-by stops for a moment,
nods to me and goes.

017 These little thoughts are the rustle of leaves;
they have their whisper of joy in my mind.

016
今天早晨，我坐在窗前，
世界宛如過客，
駐足片刻，
向我點點頭便離開了。

017
這些零碎思緒，就像樹葉的簌沙聲，
於我心坎細數歡樂。

018
你看不見真正的自己，
所見的只是你的影子。

019
主啊，我的那些願望真是癡傻，
在您的歌聲中喧嚷著。
讓我單純地靜靜聆聽吧！

020
我無法選擇最好的，
是最好的來選擇我。

018
What you are you do not see,
what you see is your shadow.

019
My wishes are fools, they shout across thy songs, my Master.
Let me but listen.

020
I cannot choose the best.
The best chooses me.

021
把燈籠提在身後的人，
將影子投在自己身前。

022
我的存在本身即屬永恆的驚喜，
這就是生命。

023
「我們這些沙沙作響的樹葉，
以聲音回應暴風雨。
但你是誰呀，如此沉默？」
「我只是一朵花兒。」

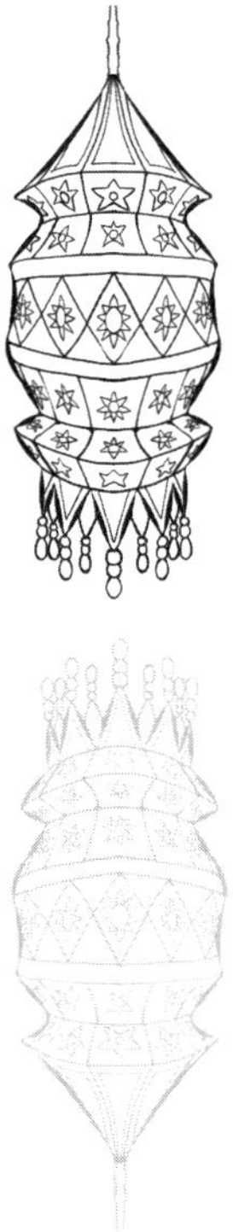

021 They throw their shadows before them
who carry their lantern on their back.

022 That I exist is a perpetual surprise
which is life.

023 "We, the rustling leaves,
have a voice that answers the storms,
but who are you so silent?"
"I am a mere flower."

024 Rest belongs to the work
as the eyelids to the eyes.

025 Man is a born child,
his power is the power of growth.

026 God expects answers for the flowers he sends us,
not for the sun and the earth.

024
休息之於工作，
正如眼瞼之於眼睛。

025
人好比初生的嬰孩，
成長的力量即為他的力量。

026
神期盼我們答謝，
乃是因為祂送了花朵給我們，
而不是因為陽光和土地。

027 The light that plays, like a naked child,
among the green leaves happily knows not that man can lie.

028 O Beauty,
find thyself in love,
not in the flattery of thy mirror.

027
光宛如赤子般快活地嬉遊於綠葉間，
殊不知人間充斥著虛偽謊言。

028
喔，美啊，
在愛中尋找你自己，
別往鏡中的阿諛裡尋。

029
我的心在世界的海岸拍擊著她的浪花，
並以眼淚署下「我愛你」這幾個字。

030
「月兒啊，你在等候什麼？」
「等著問候我該讓出路來的太陽。」

029 My heart beats her waves at the shore of the world
and writes upon it her signature in tears with the words, “ I love thee. ”

030 “ Moon, for what do you wait? ”
“ To salute the sun for whom I must make way. ”

031
綠葉伸長到我窗前，
宛如瘖啞的大地發出渴望之聲。

032
神對自己創造的清晨，
亦感到新奇無比。

033
生命因對世界的索求而致富，
因對愛的索求而有了價值。

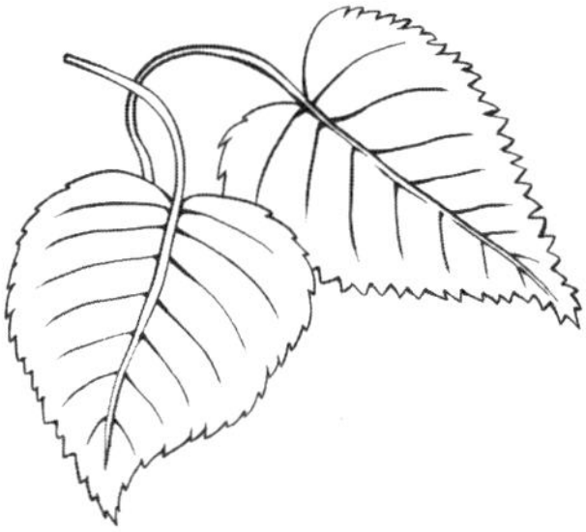

031 The trees come up to my window
like the yearning voice of the dumb earth.

032 His own mornings
are new surprises to God.

033 Life finds its wealth by the claims of the world,
and its worth by the claims of love.

034 The dry river-bed finds no thanks
for its past.

035 The bird wishes it were a cloud.
The cloud wishes it were a bird.

036 The waterfall sings,
“ I find my song, when I find my freedom. ”

034
乾涸的河床，
並不感謝它的過去。

035
鳥兒願自己是一片雲。
雲兒願自己是一隻鳥。

036
瀑布唱著：
「當我覓獲自由時，便會找到我的歌聲。」

037 I cannot tell why this heart languishes in silence.
It is for small needs it never asks, or knows or remembers.

038 Woman,
when you move about in your household service,
your limbs sing like a hill stream among its pebbles.

039 The sun goes to cross the Western sea,
leaving its last salutation to the East.

037
我不明白這心為何如此默然頹喪。
就因那些它從不問、不懂或不記得的小小需求。

038
女人哪，當你在料理家務四處移動時，
你的手足彷如在山澗溪流的小卵石間輕歌漫舞著。

039
太陽橫越西方之海時，
向東方留下他最後的問候。

040
別因自己沒胃口而抱怨食物。

041
樹群好似大地的渴望，
踮起腳尖窺向天堂。

040 Do not blame your food
because you have no appetite.

041 The trees, like the longings of the earth,
stand a-tiptoe to peep at the heaven.

042
你什麼也沒說，僅對著我微笑，
我竟覺得這就是我等候已久的。

043
水裡的魚兒是靜默的，陸上的野獸是喧鬧的，
空中的鳥兒是歡唱的。
可是，人卻兼有大海的靜默、大地的喧鬧
和天上的樂音。

042
You smiled and talked to me of nothing
and I felt that for this I had been waiting long.

043
The fish in the water is silent,
the animal on the earth is noisy,
the bird in the air is singing,
But Man has in him the silence of the sea,
the noise of the earth and the music of the air.

044 The world rushes on over the strings of the lingering heart
making the music of sadness.

045 He has made his weapons his gods.
When his weapons win he is defeated himself.

046 God finds himself
by creating.

044 世界滑過躊躇的心弦，
奏出憂傷樂曲。

045 將自己的武器視為神的人，
當武器得勝時，他卻被自己打敗了。

046 神在創造中，找到自己。

047
影子戴上她的面紗，
用她靜躡的愛之腳步，
悄柔地追隨著「光」。

048
群星不怕自己看起來像螢火蟲。

049
感謝上帝，我不是那些權力之輪，
而是被它壓輾而過的生靈之一。

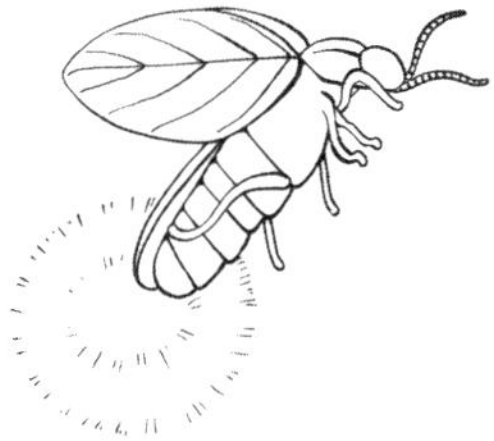

047 Shadow, with her veil drawn,
follows Light in secret meekness,
with her silent steps of love.

048 The stars are not afraid to appear
like fireflies.

049 I thank thee that I am none of the wheels of power
but I am one with the living creatures that are crushed by it.

050 The mind, sharp but not broad,
sticks at every point but does not move.

051 Your idol is shattered in the dust
to prove that God's dust is greater than your idol.

052 Man does not reveal himself in his history,
he struggles up through it.

050
心智，精明但不寬闊，
執著於每個細微末節，不知前進。

051
你的偶像消散於塵土中，
證明了神的塵土比你的偶像還偉大。

052
過往陳跡無法展現一個人，
唯可不斷奮力向前行。

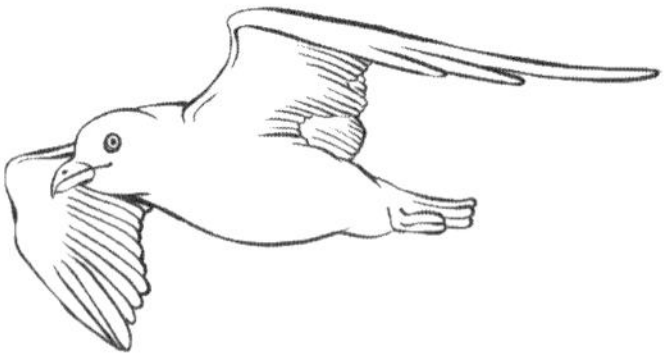

053
玻璃燈責備瓦燈擅自與之稱兄道弟，
當月亮升起時，玻璃燈卻殷勤笑著，
喚她：「我親愛，親愛的姊妹。」

054
我們就像海鷗與浪濤相遇一般，
彼此相近、相親。
海鷗紛飛，浪濤滾滾而逝，
我們也隨之分離了。

053 While the glass lamp rebukes the earthen for calling it cousin,
the moon rises, and the glass lamp,
with a bland smile, calls her, — " My dear, dear sister. "

054 Like the meeting of the seagulls and the waves
we meet and come near.
The seagulls fly off, the waves roll away and we depart.

055 My day is done,
and I am like a boat drawn on the beach,
listening to the dance-music of the tide in the evening.

056 Life is given to us,
we earn it by giving it.

057 We come nearest to the great
when we are great in humility.

055
一天的工作結束了，
我就像一艘被拖上岸的船隻，
聆聽著晚潮舞動的樂曲。

056
生命是上蒼賦予的，
唯有付出生命，才算真正得到它。

057
我們最謙卑那刻，始最接近偉大。

058 The sparrow is sorry for the peacock
at the burden of its tail.

059 Never be afraid of the moments
— thus sings the voice of the everlasting.

060 The hurricane seeks the shortest road by the no-road,
and suddenly ends its search in the Nowhere.

058
麻雀可憐孔雀得忍受自己笨重的屏尾。

059
永不畏懼「短暫的瞬間」
——永恆之聲如此唱著。

060
颶風在絕路中尋找捷徑，
卻又在絕地倏然停止搜尋。

061
就我的酒杯飲了我的酒吧，朋友。
環浮其上的泡沫一倒入別人的酒杯，
便會消失了。

062
「完美」因愛慕「不完美」，
而以美來裝扮自己。

061 Take my wine in my own cup, friend.
It loses its wreath of foam
when poured into that of others.

062 The Perfect decks itself in beauty
for the love of the Imperfect.

063
神對人類說：
「我為了治癒你而傷害你，我因愛你而懲罰你。」

064
感謝燈焰的光明，
但也別忘了堅忍站在黑暗中的燈臺啊。

063 God says to man,
" I heal you therefore I hurt, love you therefore punish. "

064 Thank the flame for its light,
but do not forget the lampholder standing
in the shade with constancy of patience.

065 Tiny grass, your steps are small,
but you possess the earth under your tread.

066 The infant flower opens its bud and cries,
" Dear World, please do not fade. "

067 God grows weary of great kingdoms,
but never of little flowers.

065 小草啊，
你的腳步雖小，卻擁有腳下的大地。

066 幼嫩的花朵綻放它的花蕾並喊道：
「親愛的世界啊，請別凋謝。」

067 神逐漸厭煩龐大的王國，
卻永不厭倦那小小的花朵。

068
邪惡經不起考驗，
正義卻可以。

069
瀑布歌唱著：
「儘管一瓢水便足以止渴，
但我卻歡歡喜喜地獻出我的全部。」

070
以不斷迸流進出的歡樂湧流，
將這些花朵拋擲而上的那座泉源在哪啊？

068 Wrong cannot afford defeat
but Right can.

069 "I give my whole water in joy," sings the waterfall,
"though little of it is enough for the thirsty."

070 Where is the fountain that throws up these flowers
in a ceaseless outbreak of ecstasy?

071 The woodcutter's axe begged for its handle from the tree.
The tree gave it.

072 In my solitude of heart I feel the sigh of
this widowed evening veiled with mist and rain.

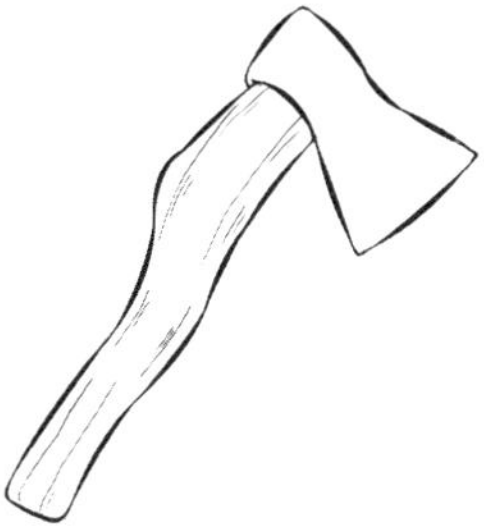

071
樵夫的斧頭向樹乞求斧柄。
樹便給了它。

072
在我孤寂的心裡，
察覺到這霧雨濛濛的孤獨夜所發出之嘆息。

073 Chastity is a wealth that comes from
abundance of love.

074 The mist, like love,
plays upon the heart of the hills
and brings out surprises of beauty.

073 貞潔是從豐盈之愛中滋養出來的財富。

074 霧，
宛如愛情，在山丘的心頭上嬉戲，
引領出種種美麗的驚喜。

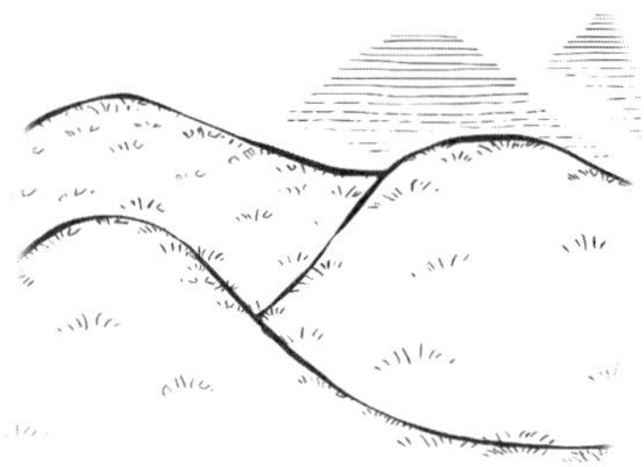

075
我們誤解了世界，
卻反控世界騙了我們。

076
詩人的風穿越海洋和森林，
追尋自己的聲音。

077
每個孩子出生，
都帶來了上帝尚未對人類失望的神諭。

075 We read the world wrong
and say that it deceives us.

076 The poet wind is out over the sea and the forest
to seek his own voice.

077 Every child comes with the message
that God is not yet discouraged of man.

078
小草在大地尋找她的夥伴。
大樹往空中尋找他的孤寂。

079
人類常對自己築起堤防。

080
我的朋友，你的話音徘徊在我心中，
就像大海的低吟，
迴盪在靜靜聆聽的松林間。

078 The grass seeks her crowd in the earth.
The tree seeks his solitude of the sky.

079 Man barricades
against himself.

080 Your voice, my friend, wanders in my heart,
like the muffled sound of the sea among these listening pines.

081 What is this unseen flame of darkness
whose sparks are the stars?

082 Let life be beautiful like summer flowers
and death like autumn leaves.

083 He who wants to do good knocks at the gate;
he who loves finds the gate open.

081
這黑暗中將火花化為繁星的隱形之火，
到底是什麼？

082
願生命如盛夏花朵般美燦，
死亡亦如秋天落葉般靜好。

083
想行善的人在門口敲著門，
想獻出愛的人會發現門已為之敞開。

084 In death the many becomes one;
in life the one becomes many.
Religion will be one when God is dead.

085 The artist is the lover of Nature,
therefore he is her slave and her master.

086 "How far are you from me, O Fruit?"
"I am hidden in your heart, O Flower."

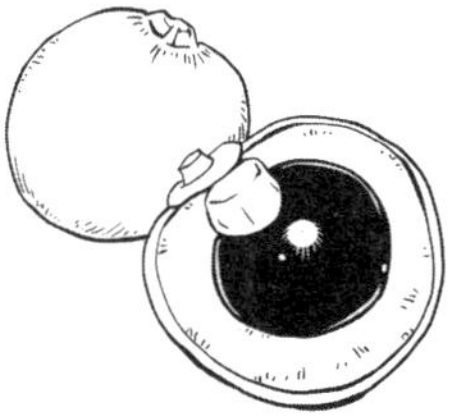

084
眾生在死中合而為一；
一在生中幻化為眾生。
當神死時，宗教終將合而為一。

085
藝術家是大自然的情人，
因此他是大自然的僕人，也是她的主人。

086
「果實啊，你離我有多遠呢？」
「花兒啊，我就藏在你心裡。」

087
這份渴念，
是那些自覺身處於黑暗中的人才感受得到，
在白晝中便無從得見。

088
露珠對湖水說：
「你是荷葉下的大露珠，我是荷葉上的小露珠。」

087 This longing is for the one who is felt in the dark,
but not seen in the day.

088 "You are the big drop of dew under the lotus leaf,
I am the smaller one on its upper side, "
said the dewdrop to the lake.

089
刀鞘為了保護刀的鋒利，
而自足於本身的駑鈍。

090
在黑暗中，「一」視若一體；
在光亮中，「一」則視若眾多樣貌。

091
在綠草的點綴下，
大地顯得宜人可居。

089 The scabbard is content to be dull
when it protects the keenness of the sword.

090 In darkness the One appears as uniform;
in the light the One appears as manifold.

091 The great earth makes herself hospitable
with the help of the grass.

092 The birth and death of the leaves
are the rapid whirls of the eddy
whose wider circles move slowly among stars.

093 Power said to the world, " You are mine. "
The world kept it prisoner on her throne.
Love said to the world, " I am thine. "
The world gave it the freedom of her house.

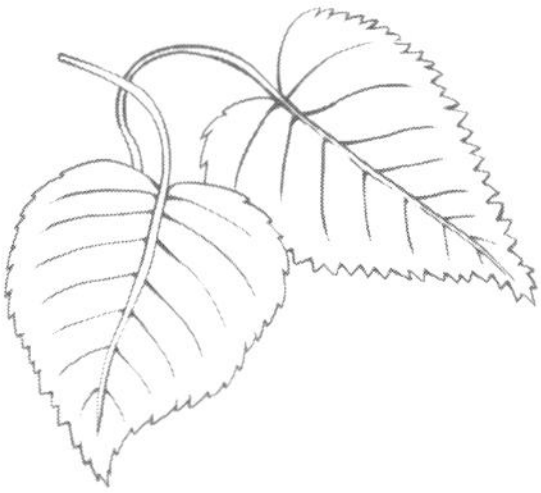

092
綠葉的生死如漩渦疾速轉動，
而較外緣的迴流，則緩行於星辰間。

093
權力對世界說：「你是我的。」
世界遂將權力囚禁於她的寶座下。
愛對世界說：「我是您的。」
世界便給了愛出入寶殿的自由。

094 The mist is like the earth's desire.
It hides the sun for whom she cries.

095 Be still, my heart,
these great trees are prayers.

096 The noise of the moment scoffs
at the music of the Eternal.

094
霧宛如大地的渴望，
當大地哭求太陽時，霧便將之藏起。

095
靜默吧，我心，
這些參天大樹都是祈禱者呢。

096
短暫時刻的喧鬧，
譏笑著永恆的音樂。

097
我想及那些浮沉於生命、
愛與死之流的過往歲月已遭遺忘，
於是我感知到離開塵世的自由。

098
我靈魂的憂傷，就像新娘的面紗，
等著午夜被掀開。

097 I think of other ages that floated upon
the stream of life and love and death and are forgotten,
and I feel the freedom of passing away.

098 The sadness of my soul is her bride's veil.
It waits to be lifted in the night.

099
死亡的印記賦予生命之幣價值，
使其能用生命換取那些真正寶貴之物。

100
白雲謙遜地站在天邊一隅。
晨曦冠之以絢麗的光輝。

099 Death's stamp gives value to the coin of life;
making it possible to buy with life what is truly precious.

100 The cloud stood humbly in a corner of the sky.
The morning crowned it with splendour.

101 The dust receives insult
and in return offers her flowers.

102 Do not linger to gather flowers to keep them, but walk on,
for flowers will keep themselves blooming all your way.

103 Roots are the branches down in the earth.
Branches are roots in the air.

101 塵土飽受玷辱，卻報之以花朵。

102 不必費心停下腳步採集花朵，
只管繼續往前走，
因為花自會隨著你的腳步開滿路。

103 根是地下的枝幹。
枝幹是空中的根。

104 The music of the far-away summer
flutters around the Autumn seeking its former nest.

105 Do not insult your friend by lending him merits
from your own pocket.

106 The touch of the nameless days clings to my heart
like mosses round the old tree.

104
早已遠逝的夏音，飄繞著秋，
尋找它舊日的巢。

105
別把你口袋裡的功勛借給友人，
那是對他的侮辱。

106
那些無名歲月裡的感觸攀附我心，
宛如攀緣在老樹上的青苔。

107
回音嘲笑她的原聲，
試以證明她才是原聲。

108
當飛黃騰達者吹噓自己得到神特別的恩寵時，
神卻為之羞愧。

107
The echo mocks her origin
to prove she is the original.

108
God is ashamed when the prosperous boasts of
His special favour.

109
之所以將自己的影子投射在前方道路上，
乃因我還有一盞未點燃的明燈。

110
人們走入喧嘩的人群，
乃為了淹沒自個兒內心沉默的吶喊聲。

109 I cast my own shadow upon my path,
because I have a lamp that has not been lighted.

110 Man goes into the noisy crowd
to drown his own clamour of silence.

111 That which ends in exhaustion is death,
but the perfect ending is in the endless.

112 The sun has his simple robe of light.
The clouds are decked with gorgeousness.

113 The hills are like shouts of children who raise their arms,
trying to catch stars.

111
枯竭的盡頭是死亡，
但圓滿的盡頭卻是永恆。

112
太陽只有一件簡樸的光袍，
雲朵卻因此披上璀璨的衣裳。

113
山群宛如叫跳著的孩子，高舉雙臂，
想要摘下星星。

114 The road is lonely in its crowd,
for it is not loved.

115 The power that boasts of its mischiefs is laughed at
by the yellow leaves that fall,
and clouds that pass by.

114
道路在熙攘人群間是寂寥的，
因為它不受人憐愛。

115
權力吹誇著自己的惡行，
卻被飄落的黃葉及路過的浮雲嘲笑。

116

今天大地在陽光下對我哼唱，

宛如紡織婦，

用一種已被遺忘的語言，吟唱著古老的歌謠。

117

草葉無愧於它所生長的偉大世界。

116

The earth hums to me to-day in the sun,
like a woman at her spinning,
some ballad of the ancient time in a forgotten tongue.

117

The grass-blade is worth of the great world
where it grows.

118
夢是嘮叨不休的妻子。
睡眠是默默忍受的丈夫。

119
夜吻著逐漸逝去的白晝，在他耳邊低語道：
「我是死亡，你的母親。
我將賦予你新生命。」

118 Dream is a wife who must talk.
Sleep is a husband who silently suffers.

119 The night kisses the fading day whispering to his ear,
"I am death, your mother. I am to give you fresh birth."

120 I feel thy beauty, dark night, like that of the loved woman
when she has put out the lamp.

121 I carry in my world that flourishes
the worlds that have failed.

120 黑夜啊，你的美，我感覺到了，
宛似暗燈下的可愛女人。

121 我在我的世界，
扛負著促成這繁榮盛世背後的諸多失敗。

122
親愛的朋友，
每當我在海灘聽著濤聲時，
便感覺到你在多少暮色漸深的黃昏裡，
所懷那些偉大思想的靜默。

123
鳥以為將魚舉到空中，是一種善舉。

122 Dear friend,
I feel the silence of your great thoughts
of many a deepening eventide on this beach
when I listen to these waves.

123 The bird thinks it is an act of kindness
to give the fish a lift in the air.

124 "In the moon thou sendest thy love letters to me,"
said the night to the sun.
"I leave my answers in tears upon the grass."

125 The Great is a born child;
when he dies he gives his great childhood to the world.

124 黑夜對太陽說：
「你在月光下將情書送給了我，
我在草地上留下淚珠作為答覆。」

125 偉大是個初生的孩子；
當他死後，將他偉大的童年留給了世界。

126 Not hammer-strokes, but dance of the water
sings the pebbles into perfection.

127 Bees sip honey from flowers and hum their thanks when they leave.
The gaudy butterfly is sure that the flowers owe thanks to him.

126
不是鎚子的錘鍊，
而是流水的舞動——
唱得卵石臻至完美。

127
蜜蜂在花叢中採蜜，離開時嗡嗡鳴謝。
美豔的蝴蝶卻理所當然認為，
花兒應向牠道謝。

128 若你不想等待以便說出完整的真理，
逞口舌之快是很容易的。

129 「可能」向「不可能」問：
「何處是你的居所？」
「無能者的夢裡。」它這麼回答道。

130 若你將所有的錯誤都關在門外，
那麼就連真理也會被屏棄在外。

128 To be outspoken is easy
when you do not wait to speak the complete truth.

129 Asks the Possible to the Impossible, " Where is your dwelling-place? "
" In the dreams of the impotent, " comes the answer.

130 If you shut your door to all errors
truth will be shut out.

131 I hear some rustle of things behind my sadness of heart,
— I cannot see them.

132 Leisure in its activity is work.
The stillness of the sea stirs in waves.

133 The leaf becomes flower when it loves.
The flower becomes fruit when it worships.

131
我聽見有東西在我憂傷的心後沙沙作響——
可我看不見它們。

132
閒暇一旦動起來便是工作。
靜止的海水一旦波動便成了浪濤。

133
葉子付出愛時，便開了花朵。
花朵崇敬神時，便成了果實。

134
地下的樹根讓樹枝結出果實，
卻不求回報。

135
這雨夜，風吹不息。
我望著搖曳的樹枝，感念萬物的偉大。

134
The roots below the earth claim no rewards for making the branches fruitful.

135
This rainy evening the wind is restless.
I look at the swaying branches and ponder over the greatness of all things.

136
午夜的暴風雨，
彷如不該在黑夜醒來的巨大孩子，
開始嬉戲喧鬧。

137
你捲起浪濤，徒然地追隨你的愛人，
啊，大海，
你這暴風雨的寂寞新娘。

136 Storm of midnight, like a giant child
awakened in the untimely dark, has begun to play and shout.

137 Thou raisest thy waves vainly to follow thy lover, O Sea,
thou lonely bride of the storm.

138 "I am ashamed of my emptiness,"
said the Word to the Work.
"I know how poor I am when I see you,"
said the Work to the Word.

139 Time is the wealth of change,
but the clock in its parody makes it mere change and no wealth.

138
「我為自己的空洞感到慚愧。」
——文字對工作這般說道。
「當我看見你，便瞭解到自己有多貧乏。」
——工作對文字如此回話。

139
時間是變化的寶藏，
然而時鐘在它拙劣的模仿中，
只生出變化卻不見寶藏。

140 Truth in her dress finds facts too tight.
In fiction she moves with ease.

141 When I travelled to here and to there,
I was tired of thee, O Road,
but now when thou leadest me to everywhere
I am wedded to thee in love.

140
「真理」穿上衣裳，卻覺事實太過束縛。
在想像中，她反倒行動自如。

141
從前我旅行到這裡、那裡時，
我厭倦了你呀，道路。
而今當你引領我走向四方時，
我在愛中與你結縭了。

142
就讓我揣想繁星中有一顆星，
引導我的生命走過那未知的黑暗吧。

143
女人，你用你優雅的手指碰觸我所有之物，
秩序便如音樂般暢流而生。

144
悲傷的聲音在已逝年華中有個巢。
它在夜裡對我唱道：「我曾愛過你。」

142
Let me think that there is one among those stars
that guides my life through the dark unknown.

143
Woman, with the grace of your fingers
you touched my things and order came out like music.

144
One sad voice has its nest among the ruins of the years.
It sings to me in the night, — " I loved you. "

145
熊熊烈火用它的灼熱警告我遠離它。
請將我從埋在灰裡的餘燼中拯救出來吧！

146
縱擁有滿天的星斗，
然而，唉，我屋裡的小燈卻沒有亮。

145
The flaming fire warns me off by its own glow.
Save me from the dying embers hidden under ashes.

146
I have my stars in the sky,
but oh for my little lamp unlit in my house.

147 The dust of the dead words clings to thee.
Wash thy soul with silence.

148 Gaps are left in life
through which comes the sad music of death.

149 The world has opened its heart of light in the morning.
Come out, my heart, with thy love to meet it.

147
已逝的文字化為塵土黏附您身。
用靜默洗滌您的靈魂吧。

148
生命留下許多缺口，
死亡的哀樂從中傳來。

149
世界在清晨敞開它光明的心。
出來吧，我心，
帶著你的愛迎向它。

150 My thoughts shimmer with these shimmering leaves
and my heart sings with the touch of this sunlight;
my life is glad to be floating with all things into the blue of space,
into the dark of time.

151 God's great power is in the gentle breeze,
not in the storm.

150
我的思緒，隨著這些閃閃發亮的葉子閃耀著；
我的心，在陽光的撫觸下歌唱著；
我的生命，因得與萬物同浮遊於穹蒼、
時間之輪裡而歡喜著。

151
上帝神威潛藏在輕柔的微風中，
而不在狂風暴雨裡。

152

這只是一場夢，
夢裡的所有事物分崩離析，緊緊壓迫著我。
待我醒來，
我將發現所有事物均完好收放在您那裡，
而我也將得到自由。

153

「誰將接下我的工作？」落日問道。
「我將盡我所能，我的主人。」瓦燈應答。

152

This is a dream in which things are all loose and they oppress.
I shall find them gathered in thee when I awake and shall be free.

153

"Who is there to take up my duties?"
asked the setting sun.
"I shall do what I can, my Master,"
said the earthen lamp.

154
摘下花瓣，
無法讓你得到花朵的美麗。

155
沉默會馱負著你的聲音，
宛似鳥巢托著歇眠的鳥兒。

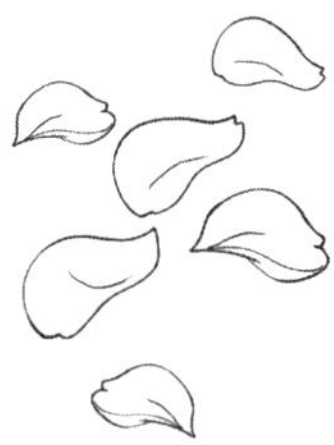

154 By plucking her petals
you do not gather the beauty of the flower.

155 Silence will carry your voice
like the nest that holds the sleeping birds.

156 The Great walks with the Small without fear.
The Middling keeps aloof.

157 The night opens the flowers in secret
and allows the day to get thanks.

158 Power takes as ingratitude the writhings of
its victims.

156
「偉大」不怕與「渺小」同行。
「平庸」卻避而遠之。

157
黑夜悄悄使花朵綻放，
卻讓白晝去接受人們的感謝。

158
「權力」視犧牲者的悲憤為忘恩負義的行為。

159 When we rejoice in our fulness,
then we can part with our fruits with joy.

160 The raindrops kissed the earth and whispered,
— " We are thy homesick children, mother,
come back to thee from the heaven. "

159 當我們因圓滿而歡喜時，
便能欣然放下我們所成就的果實。

160 雨滴親吻著大地低語：
「我們是您思鄉的孩子呀，母親，
從天上回到您身邊了。」

161
蜘蛛網假裝要抓住露珠，
卻抓到了蒼蠅。

162
愛情啊！
當你手持燃燒著痛苦的燈走來時，
我得以看見你的容顏，
並知道你就是幸福。

161 The cobweb pretends to catch dewdrops
and catches flies.

162 Love!
When you come with the burning lamp of pain in your hand,
I can see your face and know you as bliss.

163
「學者說你的光總有一天會消失。」
——螢火蟲對星星如是說道。
星星未加回答。

164
在黃昏暮色中，
某些拂曉之鳥來到我靜默之巢。

163 "The learned say that your lights will one day be no more,"
said the firefly to the stars.
The stars made no answer.

164 In the dusk of the evening
the bird of some early dawn comes to the nest of my silence.

165 Thoughts pass in my mind like flocks
of ducks in the sky.
I hear the voice of their wings.

166 The canal loves to think
that rivers exist solely to supply it with water.

165 思緒掠過心頭，猶如飛過穹蒼的一群野雁。
我聽到牠們鼓翼的聲音。

166 運河總喜歡自認為，
河流的存在只為供應它水流。

167 The world has kissed my soul with its pain,
asking for its return in songs.

168 That which oppresses me,
is it my soul trying to come out in the open,
or the soul of the world knocking at my heart for its entrance?

167 世界以其苦痛親吻我的靈魂，
竟要求我報以歌聲。

168 壓迫著我的，
是我那試圖掙脫而出的靈魂，
還是輕敲我心扉想進來的塵世之魂呢？

169 思想以它獨有的文字餵養自己，
成長茁壯。

170 我將我心之空瓶浸沒在這沉默的時刻中，
它便汲滿了愛。

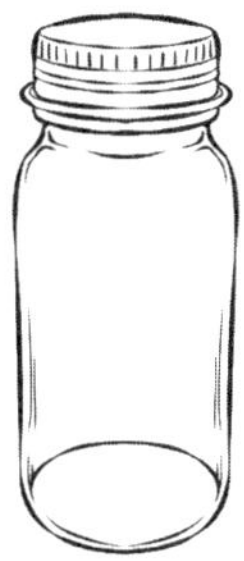

169 Thought feeds itself
with its own words and grows.

170 I have dipped the vessel of my heart into this silent hour;
it has filled with love.

171 Either you have work or you have not.
When you have to say, "Let us do something,"
then begins mischief.

172 The sunflower blushed to own the nameless flower as her kin.
The sun rose and smiled on it, saying,
"Are you well, my darling?"

171
無論你有工作，還是賦閒也好。
當你一說：「讓我們做點事吧！」
麻煩便開始出現了。

172
向日葵羞於視不知名的花為同類。
太陽冉冉升起，向不知名的花微笑道：
「你好嗎，我的寶貝？」

173

「是誰如命運般驅策我向前？」
「正是在我背後大步走著的自己啊。」

174

雲兒將水注滿河流的水杯，
自己卻隱逸在遠山中。

173

"Who drives me forward like fate?"
"The Myself striding on my back."

174

The clouds fill the water-cups of the river,
hiding themselves in the distant hills.

175
我一路走來，
水不斷從罐中潑灑而出，
最後只剩下一點點可供家用。

176
盆中的水清晰可見；
海裡的水卻黑沉無比。
小道理可以用文字話語說明白，
而大道理唯有偉大的沉默可證。

175 I spill water from my water-jar as I walk on my way.
Very little remains for my home.

176 The water in a vessel is sparkling;
the water in the sea is dark.
The small truth has words that are clear;
the great truth has great silence.

177 Your smile was the flowers of your own fields,
your talk was the rustle of your own mountain pines,
but your heart was the woman that we all know.

178 It is the little things that I leave behind for my loved ones,
— great things are for everyone.

177
你的微笑，是你自己園裡的花朵；
你的話語，是你自己山中的松濤；
但是你的心呀，
卻似我們都熟知的平常女人。

178
我留給我愛的人，只是些小東西——
偉大事物全留給大家。

179 Woman,
thou hast encircled the world's heart with
the depth of thy tears as the sea has the earth.

180 The sunshine greets me with a smile.
The rain, his sad sister, talks to my heart.

179
女人啊，
你用深深的淚水環繞著世界的心，
有如大海環繞著大地。

180
陽光以微笑向我問候。
而雨，陽光憂傷的姊妹，向我心傾訴。

181 白晝的花落下花瓣，便被遺忘了。
此花入夜便熟成為記憶的金色果實。

182 我就像夜間小徑，
在寂靜中細聽著記憶的足音。

183 薄暮天空對我來講，
就像一扇窗，一盞點亮的燈，
以及那燈後的等待。

181 My flower of the day dropped its petals forgotten.
In the evening it ripens into a golden fruit of memory.

182 I am like the road in the night
listening to the footfalls of its memories in silence.

183 The evening sky to me is like a window,
and a lighted lamp, and a waiting behind it.

184
太急於行善的人，
反而找不到時間修身養性。

185
我是秋天的雲，
空空無雨，
卻在稻熟的田裡看見我的圓滿。

184 He who is too busy doing good
finds no time to be good.

185 I am the autumn cloud, empty of rain,
see my fulness in the field of ripened rice.

186 They hated and killed and men praised them.
But God in shame hastens to hide its memory
under the green grass.

187 Toes are the fingers
that have forsaken their past.

188 Darkness travels towards light,
but blindness towards death.

186
他們憤世、殺戮，世人反竟稱頌他們。
然而上帝卻羞愧得急著將祂的記憶埋藏在青草下。

187
腳趾乃是那些拋棄過去的手指。

188
黑暗趨向光明，盲目則走向死亡。

189 The pet dog suspects the universe
for scheming to take its place.

190 Sit still, my heart, do not raise your dust.
Let the world find its way to you.

189
受人們溺寵的小狗，
疑心宇宙密謀篡奪牠的地位。

190
靜靜地坐著吧，我心，
毋須揚起你的塵土。
讓世界自己尋著它的路找向你。

191
弓對即將離弦的箭低語道：
「你的自由就是我的自由。」

192
女人啊，
你的笑聲中，
蘊涵生命之泉的樂章。

193
塞滿理智的心，猶如一把全是鋒刃的刀，
讓用它的人傷手流血。

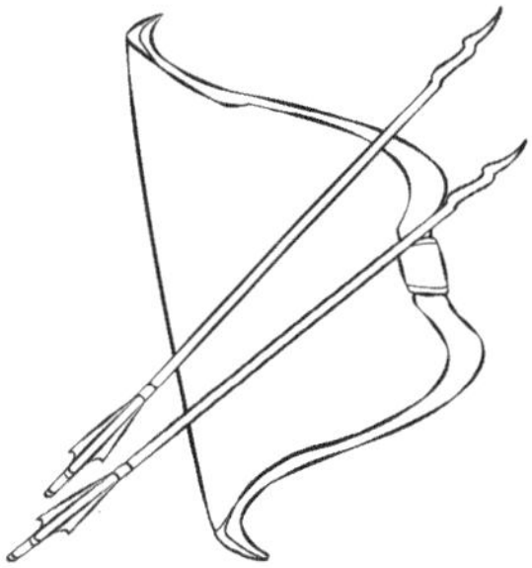

191 The bow whispers to the arrow before it speeds forth
— " Your freedom is mine. "

192 Woman, in your laughter
you have the music of the fountain of life.

193 A mind all logic is like a knife all blade.
It makes the hand bleed that uses it.

194
神喜愛人間的燈火，
尤勝於祂自己偉大的星辰。

195
這本是狂風暴雨的世界，
已被優美的音樂平服了。

196
晚霞向太陽說：
「我的心宛如收藏著您的吻的金色寶盒。」

194 God loves man's lamp lights
better than his own great stars.

195 This world is the world of wild storms
kept tame with the music of beauty.

196 "My heart is like the golden casket of thy kiss,"
said the sunset cloud to the sun.

197 By touching you may kill,
by keeping away you may possess.

198 The cricket's chirp and the patter of rain
come to me through the dark,
like the rustle of dreams from my past youth.

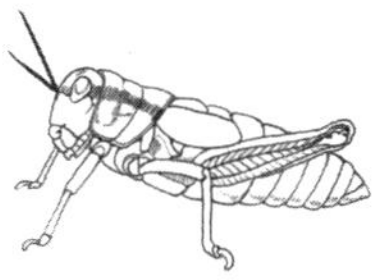

197 近距離接觸可能毀掉它，
保持距離或許能擁有它。

198 蟋蟀的唧唧聲，雨的啪嗒聲，
穿過黑暗傳到我耳邊，
彷彿是從我舊時青春夢傳來的回響。

199 "I have lost my dewdrop," cries the flower to the morning sky that has lost all its stars.

200 The burning log bursts in flame and cries, — "This is my flower, my death."

199
「我失去了我的露珠。」
——花兒向星辰落盡的晨空這般哭嚷。

200
燃燒的木頭迸出熊熊火花，
喊道：「這是我的花朵，我的死亡。」

201 黃蜂認為旁鄰蜜蜂的蜂巢太小了。
蜜蜂卻要牠造一個更小的。

202 「我留不住你的浪花，」
河岸對河流說話，
「就讓我將你的足跡留在我心裡吧。」

203 白晝，以它小小地球的喧囂，
淹沒整個宇宙的沉靜。

201 The wasp thinks that the honey-hive
of the neighbouring bees is too small.
His neighbours ask him to build one still smaller.

202 "I cannot keep your waves, " says the bank to the river.
" Let me keep your footprints in my heart. "

203 The day, with the noise of this little earth,
drowns the silence of all worlds.

204

歌聲感到空氣的無限，繪畫感到大地的無限，
而詩，則感到空氣與大地的無限；
因為詩的詞義能舞動，詩的音韻能翱翔。

205

當太陽西落，
清晨的東方已然悄立在他面前。

204 The song feels the infinite in the air,
the picture in the earth, the poem in the air and the earth;
For its words have meaning that walks and music that soars.

205 When the sun goes down to the West,
the East of his morning stands before him in silence.

206 Let me not put myself wrongly to my world
and set it against me.

207 Praise shames me,
for I secretly beg for it.

208 Let my doing nothing when I have nothing to do
become untroubled in its depth of peace like the evening
in the seashore when the water is silent.

206
別讓我有負於世界，
再拿它來對抗我。

207
讚揚使我感到羞愧，
因為我其實偷偷地希求著它。

208
當我無事可做時，讓我什麼也不做，
安詳地進入深深的平和中，
一如風平浪靜的濱海暮色。

209 Maiden, your simplicity,
like the blueness of the lake,
reveals your depth of truth.

210 The best does not come alone.
It comes with the company of the all.

209
少女啊，你的純真，
宛如湖水的藍，展現出你的淳厚。

210
至善不獨至，萬物皆相隨。

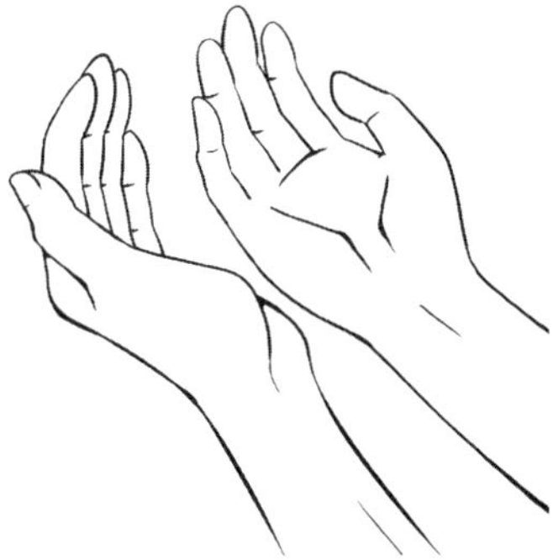

211 上帝的右手是仁慈的，
可怕的是他的左手。

註 上帝的右手代表著恩典，
左手則代表善惡的審判。

212 我的夜晚從陌生的林中走來，
說著晨星聽不懂的話語。

211 God's right hand is gentle,
but terrible is his left hand.

212 My evening came among the alien trees
and spoke in a language
which my morning stars did not know.

213 夜的黑像個袋子，
迸放出黎明的金色光芒。

214 我們的慾望將彩虹的顏色，
借給生命的煙霧。

215 神等著贏回自己的花朵，
將之當作是人類獻給祂的禮物收取。

213 Night's darkness is a bag
that bursts with the gold of the dawn.

214 Our desire lends the colours of the rainbow
to the mere mists and vapours of life.

215 God waits to win back his own flowers
as gifts from man's hands.

216 My sad thoughts tease me
asking me their own names.

217 The service of the fruit is precious,
the service of the flower is sweet,
but let my service be the service of the leaves
in its shade of humble devotion.

216
我憂傷的思緒，
一直纏著我問他們自己的名字。

217
果實的奉獻是珍貴的，
花兒的奉獻是甜美的；
然而我只想做綠葉，
卑微地奉獻一方綠蔭。

218 My heart has spread its sails to the idle winds
for the shadowy island of Anywhere.

219 Men are cruel,
but Man is kind.

218
我的心揚起帆，
乘著慵懶的風，
駛向無所不在的奇幻島。

219
群眾是殘暴的，
但人本身是善良的。

220
讓我做您的杯子吧，
將我斟滿的酒水獻給您及您的人。

221
狂風暴雨就像某個被大地拒絕了愛的天神，
在痛苦中哭喊著。

222
世界不會因為死亡而流失，
畢竟死亡並不是一條裂痕。

220 Make me thy cup and let my fulness
be for thee and for thine.

221 The storm is like the cry of some god in pain
whose love the earth refuses.

222 The world does not leak
because death is not a crack.

223 Life has become richer
by the love that has been lost.

224 My friend,
your great heart shone with the sunrise of the East
like the snowy summit of a lonely hill in the dawn.

223 生命因失去的愛情而變得更豐富。

224 我的朋友，
你偉大的心隨著東方旭日的光芒閃現，
好似黎明中的孤山雪峰。

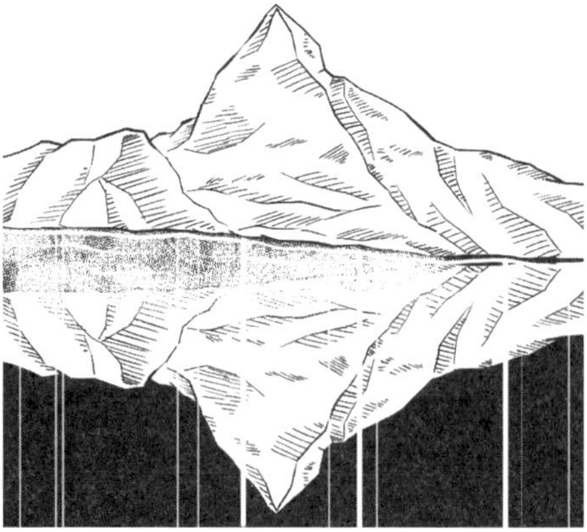

225
死亡之泉，
教生命的止水再度流動。

226
那些擁有一切唯缺您的人，
我的上帝，
嘲笑著那些一無所有但只有您的人。

227
生命的躍動，
在它自己的音樂中得到了憩息。

225
The fountain of death
makes the still water of life play.

226
Those who have everything but thee, my God,
laugh at those who have nothing but thyself.

227
The movement of life has its rest
in its own music.

228
踢腳只會揚起地上的塵土，
無法使土地長出禾米來。

229
我們的名字是夜浪中的閃閃波光，
不留任何痕跡便消逝了。

228 Kicks only raise dust and not crops
from the earth.

229 Our names are the light that glows on the sea waves at night
and then dies without leaving its signature.

230 Let him only see the thorns who has eyes
to see the rose.

231 Set the bird's wings with gold
and it will never again soar in the sky.

232 The same lotus of our clime blooms here in the alien water
with the same sweetness, under another name.

230 讓看得到玫瑰花的人，
只看到花的刺吧。

231 在鳥翼鑲上黃金，
牠便永遠無法再翱翔於穹蒼了。

232 跟我們家鄉一樣的荷花，
在這片陌生水域綻開，
同樣芬芳，只是換了個名字。

233 In heart's perspective
the distance looms large.

234 The moon has her light all over the sky,
her dark spots to herself.

233 以心透視，遠方如臨眼前。

234 月亮將她的光灑滿天際，黑點卻留給自己。

235
別說：「這是清晨。」
接著便以「昨日」之名屏棄它。
將它視為初次見面、還未有名字的新生兒吧。

236
青煙向天空誇口，
灰燼則向大地吹噓，
他們都宣稱自己是火的兄弟。

235
Do not say, " It is morning, "
and dismiss it with a name of yesterday.
See it for the first time as a new-born child
that has no name.

236
Smoke boasts to the sky, and Ashes to the earth,
that they are brothers to the fire.

237
雨滴輕聲向茉莉花說：
「請將我永遠留在你心中。」
茉莉花嘆了一聲「唉」，便墜落在地了。

238
羞怯的思緒啊，請別怕我，
我是個詩人。

237 The raindrop whispered to the jasmine,
“ Keep me in your heart for ever. ”
The jasmine sighed, “ Alas, ”
and dropped to the ground.

238 Timid thoughts, do not be afraid of me.
I am a poet.

239 The dim silence of my mind seems filled with crickets' chirp
— the grey twilight of sound.

240 Rockets, your insult to the stars
follows yourself back to the earth.

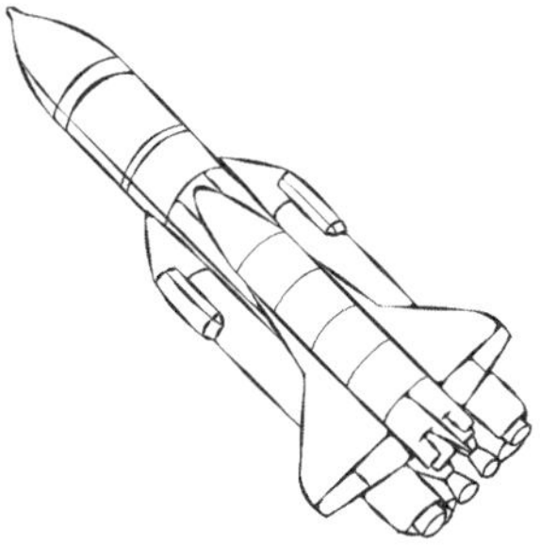

239 在我心幽微的沉默中，似乎充滿蟋蟀的唧唧聲——
有如聲音的微弱暮色。

240 火箭啊，你對星辰的侮辱，
又跟著你回到大地了。

241
您曾帶領我走過白天擁擠的旅程，
進入我日暮孤寂中。
我在夜的寂靜裡，等待著它的意義顯現。

242
生命好比橫渡海洋，
我們在同一艘狹小的船上相遇。
死亡時，你我便到岸了，
接著又各自奔向不同的世界。

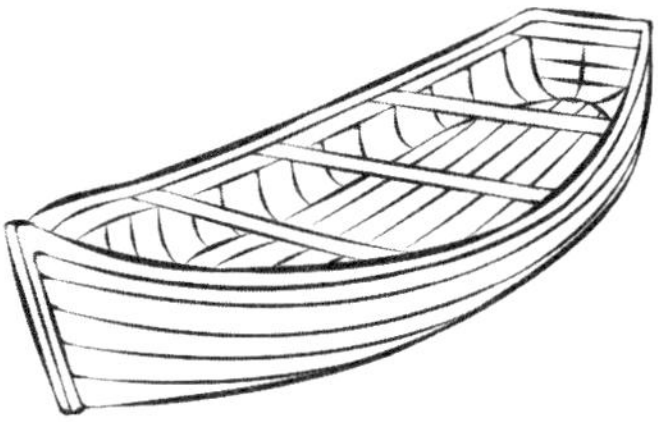

241 Thou hast led me through my crowded travels of the day
to my evening's loneliness.
I wait for its meaning through the stillness of the night.

242 This life is the crossing of a sea,
where we meet in the same narrow ship.
In death we reach the shore and go to our different worlds.

243 The stream of truth flows through
its channels of mistakes.

244 My heart is homesick to-day for the one sweet hour
across the sea of time.

243
「真理」之河，
如常流過它「錯誤」的支流。

244
今天我的心想家了，
思念跨越時間之海重返那個甜蜜時刻。

245 The bird-song is the echo of the morning light
back from the earth.

246 "Are you too proud to kiss me?"
the morning light asks the buttercup.

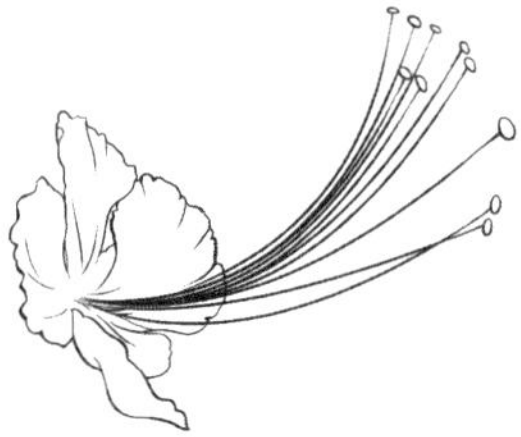

245 鳥鳴是曙光照在大地，
反射而來的回音。

246 晨光問金鳳花：
「你是否驕傲得不肯吻我？」

247
「喔，太陽，我該如何對您歌唱、崇拜您呢？」
——小花問道。
「只要用你純潔的全然靜默。」
——太陽回道。

248
當人類只是動物時，比動物還不如。

247 "How may I sing to thee and worship, O Sun?"
asked the little flower.
"By the simple silence of thy purity,"
answered the sun.

248 Man is worse than an animal
when he is an animal.

249
烏雲被光吻過後，
便成了天堂之花。

250
莫讓刀鋒嘲笑刀柄的駑鈍。

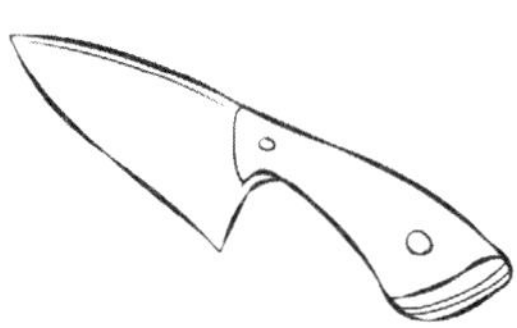

249 Dark clouds become heaven's flowers
when kissed by light.

250 Let not the sword-blade mock
its handle for being blunt.

251 The night's silence, like a deep lamp,
is burning with the light of its Milky Way.

252 Around the sunny island of Life swells day and night
death's limitless song of the sea.

251 夜的寂靜，
宛如一盞深幽的燈，燃燒著銀河之光。

252 生命猶如一座陽光島嶼，
大海日日夜夜在它周圍，
唱著無盡的死亡之歌。

253
這座山不就像一朵花，
透過它宛如花瓣的山丘，
暢享著陽光？

254
當真實的意義被曲解時，
便本末倒置，變成了「不真實」。

253 Is not this mountain like a flower,
with its petals of hills, drinking the sunlight?

254 The real with its meaning read wrong and emphasis
misplaced is the unreal.

255 Find your beauty, my heart,
from the world's movement,
like the boat that has the grace of the wind and the water.

256 The eyes are not proud of their sight
but of their eyeglasses.

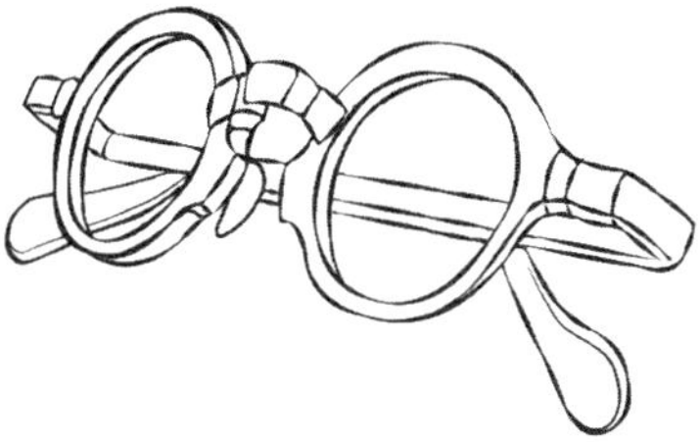

255 我的心呀，
從世界的運轉中去尋找你的美吧，
一如船擁有風與水的助力那般。

256 眼睛不以視力為傲，
卻以所戴的眼鏡自豪。

257 I live in this little world of mine and am afraid to
make it the least less.
Lift me into thy world and let me have the freedom
gladly to lose my all.

258 The false can never grow into truth
by growing in power.

257
我住在自己的小小世界裡，生怕這世界減少分毫。
把我帶到您的世界吧，
讓我擁有即使失去一切也能欣然接受的自由。

258
錯誤永遠不可能因權力的增長而變成真理。

259
我的心，渴望隨著歌聲的音韻，
輕撫這陽光燦爛的綠色世界。

260
路邊的小草啊，愛那星辰吧，
你的夢想遂即在花裡實現。

259 My heart, with its lapping waves of song,
longs to caress this green world of the sunny day.

260 Wayside grass, love the star,
then your dreams will come out in flowers.

261
讓你的音樂化身一把利劍，
穿透塵世的喧囂，直擊中心吧。

262
這棵樹顫抖的葉子，猶如嬰孩的手指，
觸動我心弦。

263
小花躺在塵土裡，
尋找著蝴蝶飛過的路徑。

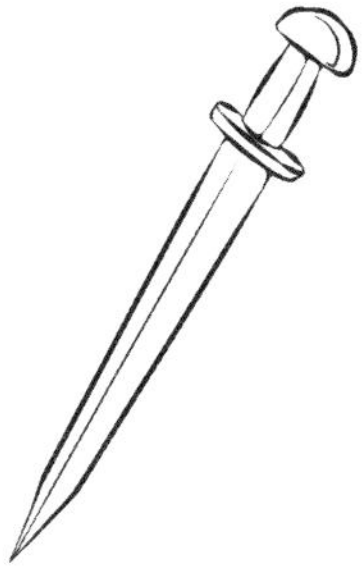

261 Let your music, like a sword,
pierce the noise of the market to its heart.

262 The trembling leaves of this tree touch my heart
like the fingers of an infant child.

263 The little flower lies in the dust.
It sought the path of the butterfly.

264 I am in the world of the roads.
The night comes. Open thy gate,
thou world of the home.

265 I have sung the songs of thy day.
In the evening
let me carry thy lamp through the stormy path.

264
我在岐路世界徘徊。
黑夜降臨了，
請打開您的門吧，
通往您如家的世界那扇門。

265
我已唱過您白晝的歌。
夜晚時，讓我拿著您的燈，
走過風雨飄搖的路吧。

266 I do not ask thee into the house.
Come into my infinite loneliness, my Lover.

267 Death belongs to life as birth does.
The walk is in the raising of the foot
as in the laying of it down.

266
我不要求你進我屋裡來。
請走進我無盡的孤寂吧，我的愛人。

267
死亡，與生一樣，都屬於生命的一部分。
舉足，與落足一樣，都是行走的一部分。

268
我已明瞭您同花兒與陽光低語的含義，
那很容易明白——
教我也明白您在痛苦與死亡中訴說的話語吧。

269
黑夜之花開遲了，當清晨親吻她時，
她顫抖又嘆息，接著便凋落在地。

270
透過萬物的哀傷，
我聽見大地之母的輕聲哼唱。

268
I have learnt the simple meaning of thy whispers
in flowers and sunshine
— teach me to know thy words in pain and death.

269
The night's flower was late when the morning kissed her,
she shivered and sighed and dropped to the ground.

270
Through the sadness of all things
I hear the crooning of the Eternal Mother.

271
大地啊，我以陌生人的身分來到你岸邊，
以客人的身分住在你屋裡，
今時則以朋友的身分走出你家門。

272
待我離去，讓我的思想陪伴著你，
就像日落餘暉，依傍在寂靜星空的邊緣。

271 I came to your shore as a stranger,
I lived in your house as a guest,
I leave your door as a friend, my earth.

272 Let my thoughts come to you, when I am gone,
like the afterglow of sunset at the margin of starry silence.

273 Light in my heart the evening star of rest
and then let the night whisper to me of love.

274 I am a child in the dark.
I stretch my hands through the coverlet of night for thee,
Mother.

273 在我心底點亮那顆晚安的星辰，
再讓黑夜向我低訴愛吧。

274 我是迷失在暗夜中的孩子。
我從重重夜幕中向您伸出雙手，母親。

275 The day of work is done. Hide my face
in your arms, Mother.
Let me dream.

276 The lamp of meeting burns long;
it goes out in a moment at the parting.

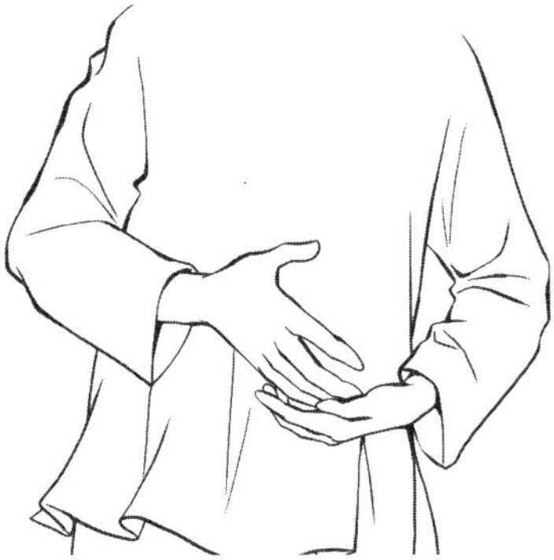

275 一天的工作結束了，
讓我將臉埋進您臂彎吧，母親。
讓我墜入夢鄉。

276 相聚時的燈光，不覺長明；
唯離別時，恍覺滅於一瞬。

277
喔，世界啊，當我死去時，
請在您的沉寂中替我留下一句話：
「我已然愛過。」

278
當我們愛這個世界時，
才算真正活在這個世界上。

279
讓死者享有不朽之名，
但讓生者擁有不滅之愛。

277
One word keep for me in thy silence,
O World, when I am dead, " I have loved. "

278
We live in this world
when we love it.

279
Let the dead have the immortality of fame,
but the living the immortality of love.

280
我曾見到您，
就像半睡半醒的孩子在黎明微光中看到母親那樣，
接著笑了笑，便又睡著了。

281
我將一次又一次死去，
好去明白生命的無窮無盡。

280
I have seen thee as the half-awakened child sees
his mother in the dusk of the dawn
and then smiles and sleeps again.

281
I shall die again and again
to know that life is inexhaustible.

282 While I was passing with the crowd in the road
I saw thy smile from the balcony
and I sang and forgot all noise.

283 Love is life in its fulness
like the cup with its wine.

282

當我隨擁擠人潮走在路上時，
看見您從陽臺上投過來的微笑，
引使我哼著歌，忘卻一切煩囂。

283

愛是圓滿的生命，
就像盛滿了酒的酒杯。

284 They light their own lamps and sing their own words
in their temples.
But the birds sing thy name in thine own morning light,
— for thy name is joy.

285 Lead me in the centre of thy silence
to fill my heart with songs.

284
他們在自己的廟裡，
點燃自己的燈，吟唱著自己的歌。
但是鳥兒卻在您的晨光裡，唱著您的名——
因為您的名便是喜樂。

285
引領我到您沉靜的中心，
好使我的心充滿歌聲。

286
就讓他們活在自己所選的燦爛煙火世界中吧。
我的心只渴望您的星光呀，我的上帝。

287
愛的痛苦圍困著我的生命悲吟，
彷如深不可測的大海；
而愛的喜悅就像鳥兒在花叢中歡唱。

286 Let them live who choose in their own hissing world of fireworks.
My heart longs for thy stars, my God.

287 Love's pain sang round my life like the unplumbed sea,
and love's joy sang like birds in its flowering groves.

288
假如您想的話，就把燈捻熄了吧。
我將瞭解您的黑暗，也會愛著它。

289
當白日將盡，我站在您面前時，
您將看見我的傷疤，
並明白我也有過創傷與業已癒合的傷口。

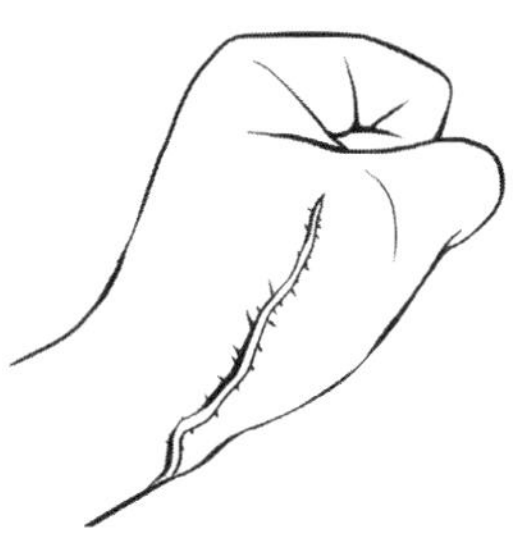

288
Put out the lamp when thou wishest.
I shall know thy darkness and shall love it.

289
When I stand before thee at the day's end
thou shalt see my scars and know that
I had my wounds and also my healing.

290 Some day I shall sing to thee
in the sunrise of some other world,
" I have seen thee before in the light of the earth,
in the love of man. "

291 Clouds come floating into my life from other days
no longer to shed rain or usher storm
but to give colour to my sunset sky.

290
總有一天，
我會在另一個世界的旭日下對您歌唱：
「我曾在地球的光裡，在人類的愛裡，見過您。」

291
往日的浮雲飄進我生命裡，
不再滴雨或興起風暴，
只是為我日夕穹空添上一抹彩霞。

292 Truth raises against itself the storm that scatters
its seeds broadcast.

293 The storm of the last night
has crowned this morning with golden peace.

292
真理激起對抗它的風暴，
風暴反將真理的種子散播開來。

293
昨夜的風暴，
為今日曉晨戴上了金色的寧和之冠。

294

真理似乎總在它最後的話語中顯現；
而這最後的話語又衍生出下一個真理。

295

他是有福之人，
因其外在名聲的光環未掩蓋過他的真實。

296

當我忘記自己的名時，
您名字的甜美總充滿我心——
宛如濛霧消失後的晨曦。

294 Truth seems to come with its final word;
and the final word gives birth to its next.

295 Blessed is he
whose fame does not outshine his truth.

296 Sweetness of thy name fills my heart when I forget mine
— like thy morning sun when the mist is melted.

297
靜謐的黑夜有著母親的美，
喧鬧的白晝則有孩子的美。

298
人微笑時，世界愛他；
人大笑時，世界便怕他了。

297 The silent night has the beauty of the mother
and the clamorous day of the child.

298 The world loved man when he smiled.
The world became afraid of him when he laughed.

299 God waits for man to regain
his childhood in wisdom.

300 Let me feel this world as thy love taking form,
then my love will help it.

301 Thy sunshine smiles upon the winter days of my heart,
never doubting of its spring flowers.

299 神靜待世人在智慧中重拾童年。

300 讓我感知這世界是您愛的體現，
那麼我也將用愛來幫助這世界。

301 您的陽光對我心裡的寒冬綻出微笑，
從不懷疑它也有春日花朵。

302 God kisses the finite in His love
and man the infinite.

303 Thou crossest desert lands of barren years
to reach the moment of fulfilment.

302
神在愛中親吻世人之「有限」，
而人則親吻神之「無限」。

303
您穿越荒蕪歲月中無數的漠地，
終抵圓滿的那一刻。

304
神的靜默，
使人的思想成熟為語言。

305
「永恆的旅人呀」，
您將在我的歌聲中，覓得您留下的足跡。

306
父親，
將您的光輝展現在您的孩子身上，
讓我不致使您蒙羞。

304 God's silence
ripens man's thoughts into speech.

305 Thou wilt find,
Eternal Traveller,
marks of thy footsteps across my songs.

306 Let me not shame thee, Father,
who displayest thy glory in thy children.

307

這是個慘淡無趣的日子，
烏雲下的光，就像被處罰的孩子，
蒼白的臉上掛著淚痕；
而風的咆哮，彷如受傷世界的哭嚎聲。
但是我知道，
自己正踏在會見摯友的路上。

307

Cheerless is the day,
 the light under frowning clouds is like a punished child
 with traces of tears on its pale cheeks,
 and the cry of the wind is like the cry of a wounded world.
But I know I am travelling to meet my Friend.

308 To-night there is a stir among the palm leaves,
a swell in the sea, Full Moon,
like the heart-throb of the world.
From what unknown sky hast thou carried
in thy silence the aching secret of love?

309 I dream of a star, an island of light,
where I shall be born
and in the depth of its quickening leisure
my life will ripen its works
like the rice-field in the autumn sun.

308
今晚，棕櫚葉生起一陣騷動，
海面忽起一陣洶湧，
滿月，就像世界之心的悸動。
您從哪個未知的天空，
默默揹來愛的痛苦秘密？

309
我夢見一顆星，那是座光明之島，
我將在那裡出生；
在那充滿活力又深幽無擾之地，
我的生命將完成它的使命，
就像秋陽下的稻田。

310 The smell of the wet earth in the rain
rises like a great chant of praise
from the voiceless multitude of the insignificant.

311 That love can ever lose
is a fact that we cannot accept as truth.

310 雨中濕土的氣息，
宛如由一群沉默平民大眾口中合唱出的偉大頌歌。

311 「愛情也可能會失去」，
乃是我們無法將之視為真理接受的事實。

312 總有一天我們會明白，
死亡永遠奪不走我們心靈獲得的東西——
因為心靈獲得的東西已與她結成一體。

313 神在屬於我的黃昏暮色中，
帶著我過去的花朵來到這兒，
而這些花兒在祂的籃子中，依然保持鮮麗。

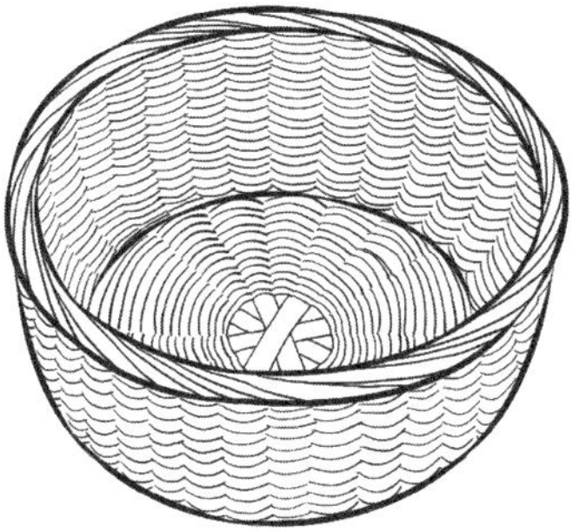

312 We shall know some day that death can
never rob us of that which our soul has gained,
for her gains are one with herself.

313 God comes to me in the dusk of my evening
with the flowers from my past kept fresh in His basket.

314 主啊，當我將生命之弦都調好音後，
您的每一次觸動，便會奏出愛的樂音。

315 我的主啊，讓我真實地活著吧，
這麼一來，死亡對我也會變得真實。

316 人類的歷史，
耐心地等候著受辱者勝利那一天。

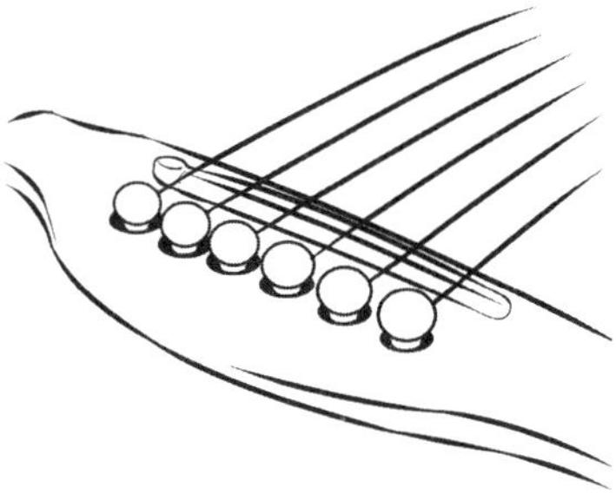

314 When all the strings of my life will be tuned, my Master,
then at every touch of thine will come out the music of love.

315 Let me live truly, my Lord,
so that death to me become true.

316 Man's history is waiting in patience
for the triumph of the insulted man.

317 I feel thy gaze upon my heart this moment
like the sunny silence of the morning
upon the lonely field whose harvest is over.

318 I long for the Island of Songs across
this heaving Sea of Shouts.

317 我感覺到此刻您正凝視著我的心，
猶如清晨沉靜旭光，
灑落在收成後的寂寥田野上。

318 我渴望渡過這洶湧的「咆哮之海」，
抵達「歌之島」。

319 The prelude of the night is commenced
in the music of the sunset,
in its solemn hymn to the ineffable dark.

320 I have scaled the peak and found no shelter
in fame's bleak and barren height.
Lead me, my Guide, before the light fades,
into the valley of quiet where life's harvest mellows
into golden wisdom.

319
夜以落日之音揭開序曲，
對其無以言喻的黑暗，
吟唱著神聖頌歌。

320
我曾登上高峰，
發現大名鼎鼎的貧脊荒蕪高處，
毫無遮蔽之地。
我的嚮導呀，在光消逝之前，
引領我到寧靜的山谷吧！
在那兒，
生命的收穫將熟成為金黃色的智慧。

321

在薄暮的灰朦中，
一切事物都顯得如此詭譎——
尖塔的底層消失於黑暗中，
樹梢宛如斑斑墨漬。
我將等待清晨醒來時，
睹見您光明中的城市。

321

Things look phantastic in this dimness of the dusk
— the spires whose bases are lost in the dark
and tree-tops like blots of ink.
I shall wait for the morning and wake up
to see thy city in the light.

322
我曾經歷過苦難及絕望，
亦曾體見過死亡，
而今何其欣喜自己活在這偉大的世界中。

323
在我的生命中，
有些荒涼寂靜的地帶。
那是我忙碌的日子裡，
汲取陽光與空氣的開闊之處。

322
I have suffered and despaired and known death
and I am glad that I am in this great world.

323
There are tracts in my life that are bare and silent.
They are the open spaces
where my busy days had their light and air.

324 Release me from my unfulfilled past clinging to me
from behind making death difficult.

325 Let this be my last word,
that I trust in thy love.

324 讓我從不圓滿的過去中解脫吧！
過去的種種，從身後緊緊糾纏著我，
讓死亡也變得困難。

325 就以這句話作為我的結語吧：
「我信您的愛。」

國家圖書館出版品預行編目資料

漂鳥集【全新插畫雙語版】／泰戈爾原著；伍晴文譯
.
——二版 . ——臺中市：好讀 , 2023.04
面：　公分，——（典藏經典；63）

譯自：Stray Birds

ISBN 978-986-178-658-2（平裝）

867.51　　112007265

好讀出版

典藏經典 63

漂鳥集【全新插畫雙語版】

作　者／泰戈爾
譯　者／伍晴文
內頁繪圖／許承菱
總 編 輯／鄧茵茵
文字編輯／莊銘桓
行銷企畫／劉恩綺
發 行 所／好讀出版有限公司
台中市 407 西屯區工業 30 路 1 號
台中市 407 西屯區大有街 13 號（編輯部）
TEL:04-23157795 FAX:04-23144188 http://howdo.morningstar.com.tw
（如對本書編輯或內容有意見，請來電或上網告訴我們）
法律顧問　陳思成律師

讀者服務專線／ TEL：02-23672044 / 04-23595819#212
讀者傳真專線／ FAX：02-23635741 / 04-23595493
讀者專用信箱／ E-mail：service@morningstar.com.tw
網路書店／ http : //www.morningstar.com.tw
郵政劃撥／ 15060393（知己圖書股份有限公司）
印刷／上好印刷股份有限公司
如有破損或裝訂錯誤，請寄回知己圖書更換

初版／西元 2014 年 8 月 1 日
二版／西元 2023 年 4 月 15 日
定價：200 元

Published by How-Do Publishing Co., Ltd.
2023 Printed in Taiwan

ISBN 978-986-178-658-2